This book belongs to

This is a Parragon book
This edition published in 2006

Parragon
Queen Street House
4 Queen Street
Bath BA1 1HE, UK

Copyright © Parragon Books Ltd 2005

ISBN 1-40545-035-5
Printed in China

My Little Angel

Written by Beth Roberts

Illustrated by Caroline Jayne Church

Lizzie was a pretty little girl
who lived with her mum,
her dad and her baby
brother Matthew.

Lizzie had bright eyes,
chestnut-brown hair
and rosy cheeks.
She looked as good and
as sweet as a little angel.

Lizzie didn't always act like an angel. In fact, sometimes she could be very naughty indeed.

One day, Lizzie was naughtier than she'd ever been before. In the morning, she decided to play with her toys. Lizzie got out her dolls and crayons. Next she got out her building blocks, and then her tea set.

Soon, Lizzie's toys were spread all over the floor.
By lunchtime, Lizzie had made a lot of mess.
"Please tidy your toys now, Lizzie," said Mum.
"No!" Lizzie said. "I don't want to!"
So Mum had to tidy everything away all by herself.

That afternoon, Lizzie's grandma came for tea.
Grandma was very pleased to see Lizzie and baby Matthew.
"Lizzie, please kiss your grandma hello," said Mum.
But Lizzie ran away from Grandma into the garden.

Lizzie peeped through the window and saw everyone enjoying lots of delicious food without her. She wished she hadn't been so rude. Instead of saying she was sorry, Lizzie stayed in the garden and sulked.

Later that evening, after Grandma had gone home, Lizzie wanted to play.
"Please play quietly, Lizzie," Mum said. "Matthew is asleep."
But Lizzie started jumping loudly across the floor.
STAMP! STAMP! STAMP! went Lizzie's feet.

Matthew woke up and began to cry.

"Stop crying, Matthew," ordered Lizzie.

She pulled a face at him. Matthew cried even harder.

"Lizzie, please be nice to Matthew," Mum said.

Lizzie stuck out her tongue rudely.

That night, as her mother tucked her into bed and kissed her goodnight, Lizzie felt unhappy. She thought about all the naughty things she'd done and wished she could make everything alright.

Soon Lizzie's eyes began to feel heavy, and a minute later she fell fast asleep.

In the middle of the night,
Lizzie was dreaming peacefully.
Suddenly, a strange glow
filled the room.
Lizzie opened her eyes
and next to her bed was a beautiful
angel. The angel had a kind face
and shimmering wings. She was
glowing with a golden light.

"Hello, Lizzie," smiled the angel. "Don't be afraid. I know that you're feeling a bit sad. I've come to try and help you."

"Who are you?" Lizzie whispered.

"I'm your friend," replied the angel. She took Lizzie by the hand.

"Let's talk about all the things that have happened today, and think about how we could have made them better. Tidying up toys isn't much fun, is it?"

Lizzie shook her head.

"But if you don't tidy up, people can hurt themselves falling over toys on the floor," said the angel.

Lizzie smiled. "I want to help Mum. I'll try and put my things away from now on," she said.

"Why did you run away from your grandma?" asked the angel. "It would make her so happy if you would spend time with her. You could have a lot of fun together."

"And what about baby Matthew?" continued the angel. "If you accidentally wake him up, why don't you try and make him laugh instead of cry?"

Lizzie nodded her head happily. That was a good idea. Lizzie felt much better.

The angel tucked Lizzie back into bed and stroked her face tenderly.

"I wish I could be a beautiful angel like you one day," Lizzie whispered.

The angel smiled. "Well, Lizzie, you have to be very good to become an angel," she replied. "But I'm sure you can do it if you try."

Lizzie nodded. "Yes, I think I can," she said. "I'll be much nicer from now on."

When Lizzie woke up the next morning, she remembered the angel's visit.

"Today I'll be different," Lizzie thought. "I'm going to try and be good all day long."

In the morning, Lizzie played with her toys.
She spread them all over the floor, and made a lot of mess.
"Please tidy up your toys now, Lizzie," Mum said.
Lizzie was about to shake her head and say that she didn't want to.

But then she remembered
what the angel had told her
about helping Mum.

Lizzie put everything away
neatly in her toy box.

"Thank you, Lizzie,"
Mum said, smiling.
"What a good girl you are!"

That afternoon, Grandma came to tea.
Without being asked, Lizzie ran up
to her and gave her a big kiss.
"Hello, Lizzie!" said Grandma
happily. "It's lovely to see you."

Lizzie and Grandma had a wonderful time. Lizzie drew Grandma a special picture, which she was very pleased with. Then they played lots of fun games together.

That evening, after Grandma had gone home, Lizzie wanted to play.
"Please play quietly," said Mum. "Matthew's sleeping."
Lizzie wanted to play noisily. She started to jump across the floor,
but then she remembered what the angel had said.

Matthew hadn't woken up, so Lizzie tiptoed silently across the room and chose a book from the shelf. She sat quietly on a bean bag to look at it. Lizzie didn't make a single sound.

As the days and weeks passed by, Lizzie was hardly naughty at all.

One day, Mum and Dad had a special surprise for her.

"We're very proud of you," said Dad, giving Lizzie a big hug. "You've been such a good girl lately that we've bought you a present."

Dad handed Lizzie a small box. Inside was a beautiful silver necklace. There was an angel charm hanging from it.

"A little angel for our little angel," said Mum.
She put the necklace around Lizzie's neck.
"Oh! Thank you!" beamed Lizzie,
as Mum gave her a great big hug.